D1685452

What any author wants is for his books to become dog-eared and familiar. I've been lucky enough that my very young readers are particularly adept at giving their books doggy ears in no time at all.

And of all my books, perhaps it's those about Kipper that get the doggiest ears of all, which I guess is kind of appropriate.

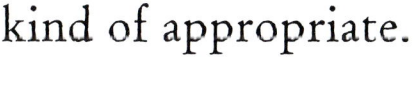

More books about Kipper

Kipper
Kipper's Toybox
Kipper's Birthday
Kipper's Snowy Day
Kipper's Christmas Eve
Kipper's A to Z
Kipper and Roly
Kipper's Monster
One Year with Kipper
Hide Me, Kipper
Kipper Story Collection
Kipper's Birthday
and Other Stories
Kipper's Little Friends

First published in 2003
by Hodder Children's Books

This edition published in 2015

Text and illustrations copyright © Mick Inkpen 2003

Hodder Children's Books
An imprint of Hachette Children's Group
Part of Hodder & Stoughton
Carmelite House
50 Victoria Embankment
London EC4Y 0DZ

The right of Mick Inkpen to be identified as the
author and the illustrator of this Work has been
asserted by him in accordance with the Copyright,
Designs and Patents Act 1988.

All rights reserved

A catalogue record of this book is available
from the British Library.

· ISBN: 978 1 444 93701 5
10 9 8 7 6 5 4 3

Printed in China

Hodder Children's Books is a division of
Hachette Children's Books.
An Hachette UK Company.

www.hachette.co.uk

Kipper's Beach Ball

Mick Inkpen

Hodder
Children's
Books

One morning as Kipper was pouring out his cornflakes, a thing dropped into his bowl, a colourful, wrinkly sort of thing.

Kipper picked up the thing and looked at it. He sniffed it. It had a nice, plasticky sort of smell.

It was quite exciting really, except that Kipper had no idea what the wrinkly, plasticky thing might be.

He hurried round to Tiger's house. 'I got a free gift in my cornflakes!' he said.

Tiger was unimpressed.

'Oh, I've been collecting them for weeks,' he said. 'I've already got the penguin rubber that goes on the end of your pencil, the wind-up shark that goes in the bath, and TWO jumpy frogs. They're just for fun. The only one I haven't got yet is the ball. What's yours then?'

Kipper held up the thing.
'It must be the ball!' he said.
It didn't look much like a ball.
It didn't look much like anything.
   'I thought balls were supposed
to be round and bouncy,' said Tiger.
   Kipper bounced the thing.
Or rather he didn't, because the
thing just hit the floor with a little
'plap!' and no bounce at all.
   It lay there looking colourful,
but useless.

It was then that they discovered the nozzle.
'Oh!' said Tiger.
'You're meant to blow it up! This isn't just an ordinary ball! It's a beach ball!'
He started to blow it up.
He blew,
and blew,
and blew,
until he became giddy and Kipper had to take over.
Slowly the wrinkly, plasticky thing turned into the fattest, shiniest, beachiest ball they had ever seen!

'**W**ow!' said Kipper.
He bounced the ball
as hard as he could.

'Wow!'
said Tiger.

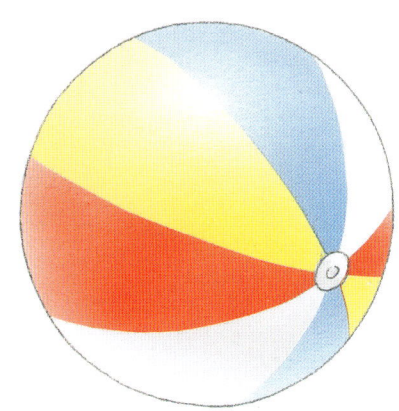

Where would you take a beach ball? To the beach, of course. And that is what they did.

Kipper was so excited as they reached the cliff top, he forgot how windy cliff tops are and threw the ball up into the air. This was a mistake.

The wind grabbed the ball and whisked it away!

It sailed high out over the beach, circling in the air, making the seagulls squawk.

Then it dropped on to the hard sand and bounced up again, spinning faster and faster away from them.

'Stop!' called Kipper, chasing down the cliff steps. But the ball rushed away.

It looped and bounced and skidded along the beach, knocking the top off a sandcastle.

And just as it seemed that it would never, never stop. . .

The sea grabbed it. And for a moment it stopped spinning, as if to catch its breath, before a wave whooshed up the beach and sucked it out into the surf.

'Come back!' shouted Kipper. But by the time Kipper and Tiger reached the water's edge, the ball was bobbing far out among the waves.

'Come back!'

And strangely, the ball seemed to do as it was told.

For at that moment a great breaking wave came looming up behind it, flicked it up on to its nose like a seal, and began bringing it back to the beach.

'It's coming! It's coming!' screamed Tiger. 'Get ready, Kipper!'

There was no time to get ready.

Kipper just hurled himself at the ball as the giant wave crashed on to the beach.

He grabbed, and disappeared in a great splash of foam and water!

But over the sound of the waves, and of the tumbling of the pebbles, and of the bubbling of the water in his ears, Kipper heard another sound, a faint pop. And he felt something collapse underneath him.

As Kipper lifted his beach ball out of the water. . .

. . .it seemed to give a sigh, and slowly it became a wrinkly thing again.

'It's sort of died!' he said to Tiger, which made them both laugh.

They tried blowing it up again, but the big split on one side let the air out as fast as they could blow.

Kipper noticed that it smelt more plasticky than ever, which for some reason made him feel suddenly sad.

'We could always buy some more cornflakes,' suggested Tiger.

So they hurried home to buy more cornflakes and ran all the way to Kipper's house with six whole boxes, which they emptied straight on to the floor. But all they found was
three penguin rubbers,
two wind-up sharks,
one jumpy frog
and lots of cornflakes.

Over the next three weeks Kipper ate nothing but cornflakes. Cornflakes for breakfast and cornflakes for dinner too. But there was no beach ball and, in the end, Kipper stopped looking.

Even so, each time he gets a new box of cornflakes Kipper sniffs the box before opening it, just in case there is a nice, plasticky sort of smell coming from inside.

'My children absolutely LOVE all of Mick Inkpen's books, and I still love reading Kipper to them, even when it's for the hundredth time...'

CRESSIDA COWELL

'He is the perfect pup to grow up with...'

HILARY McKAY

'Storytelling at its best.' DAVID MELLING